JASON ANSPACH   NICK COLE

TIN MAN

GALAXY'S EDGE

NOVA

Galaxy's Edge: TIN MAN
By Jason Anspach & Nick Cole

Text Copyright 2017, Galaxy's Edge, LLC
Print Copyright 2023, WarGate Nova
All rights reserved.

Print ISBN: 9798889220039
All rights reserved. Version 1.0
Printed in USA

Edited by David Gatewood
Published by Galaxy's Edge, LLC

Cover Art: Fabian Saravia
Cover Design: M.S. Corley
Interior Layout: Kevin G. Summers

For more information:

Website: GalaxysEdge.us
Facebook: facebook.com/atgalaxysedge
Newsletter: InTheLegion.com

DAY ONE

The Battle of the Aachon Valley took place in the northern highlands on Psydon, out along the spiral arm of the Milky Way in the long years after the end of the Savage Wars. The galactic-wide conflict was finally, definitively, over, but before the irradiated superstructures of ruined Savage cruisers could even stop glowing, the galaxy erupted into hundreds of brushfire conflicts. Long-held grudges, and grievances that had been left simmering in favor of the more imminent problem of the Savage Wars, at once determined that the time to settle up was now.

The Third Legion Expeditionary Force under the command of General Maar had been dispatched to quell the revolt on Psydon. Its legionnaires quickly found themselves in well over their bucketed heads. The entire planet had fallen under the gaze of a hypnotic rebel demagogue who argued that all taxation was theft, especially the high rate demanded by the Galactic Republic. "An outrageous level of robbery that could only be achieved by a government," he was often heard to say.

The message proved to be popular.

Reese made it back to his pre-fab cans at firebase Mojo sometime before midnight. As the ground crew taxied his bird into the maintenance hangar, he could still hear the Psydon Doro rebels shelling the hell out of the jungle, and underneath that were the sounds of heavy automatic blaster fire in sudden streaming bursts.

The Doro were coming out into the night to take the fight to the legionnaires. Reese would sleep, safe and secure, but the leejes out there wouldn't be so lucky. A few of them might be dead by dawn, their bodies waiting for him to come get them at first light.

You don't make night runs for the dead.

Reese went to the supply module and pulled out some rags, a bucket, and cleaning solution. He returned to his ship, Angel 26, back in the maintenance hangar. Already the techs were patching the blaster holes and cannibalizing the hangar queens for more parts. All had to be ready again by dawn.

"You'd better work on fixing the thrust ailerons and yaw stabilizers first," Reese called out to the techs. "They went bad halfway through the day."

When the maintenance chief saw Captain Reese with a bucket in one hand and rags and solution in the other, he efficiently stepped in the way to cut Reese off before he could climb into the cockpit.

"No sir," he said. "That's our job. We'll take care of it."

Reese stopped, staring hard at the man.

"No, it was my job," he said. "I was supposed to take care of him. I'll clean up his blood and..."

Brains.

There had been brains all over that side of the cockpit glass. Reese hadn't been able to take his eyes off it.

"... and everything else, too," he finished.

The chief nodded once, but didn't let the captain pass. "I know that, sir. We'll... take care of him, sir. It's our job. It's what we do. Let us do our jobs, sir."

And so Reese surrendered. Too tired to fight. The truth was, he'd never been a fighter. And how one ended up in the Republic Marines by not being a fighter was a mystery he never could quite figure out.

It had never really been up to him anyway. Personnel knew best. And they'd made him a medical SLIC pilot. Just like that. As though personnel had some kind of infinite wisdom that guided it through a galaxy that made less and less sense every day.

Back at his prefab, he sat down on his cot and pulled out the Faldaren scotch that he and Doger—whose brains decorated his SLIC's window—always kept for post mission "debriefs." Something between just the two of them. He splashed some into each of their canteen cups, picked up his own cup, and drank. Then he poured some more.

Reese sniffed and assessed the room. They'd already come and taken Doger's belongings away. There was just an empty cot, a tiny bare desk, the cup, and his friend's half of the scotch.

Reese pulled out his datapad and brought up some music.

Classical. Ancient music. From back when man had been something different. Back before the galaxy opened up. That was what he would listen to. Doger had hated it. Everyone had hated it. But ever since Reese took an archaic classical music appreciation class back in college, he'd been hooked. He scrolled through his list, looking at all the ancient songs. To so many in the galaxy, these symphonies and sonatas were now meaningless. But once, long ago, they had meant something.

He landed on a song that seemed right. Not a favorite, but the right choice, its words and melancholy promising to express what he felt. Or didn't feel. He was empty. He was alone.

He clicked play. And there in the tent, in the dark, as the buzz ships went out on their night missions to kill as many of the enemy as they could, while dug-in legionnaires hunkered beneath typhoons of distant artillery reaching out to land atop them on their hill forts, as someone somewhere transported what had been his co-pilot onto a ship heading back to the core, an ancient musical group known as America began to sing about a "Horse with No Name." He listened to all the old and lost songs from another time and place—not the one where he found himself.

DAY TWO

Captain Reese awoke before dawn. Already the first SLICS were up, on recon flights capable of swift strikes before the Doro disappeared back into their jungle hideouts. These SLICs would be the first to see what the battlefield looked like. Next would be the gunships, going out to kill in adult-sized doses. And then the medical SLICS to get any dead or walking wounded.

Reese drank his breakfast. More of the scotch. He wasn't hungry. He suited up, cleaned up as best he could, and made his way to flight ops.

"I'd tell you that you don't have to go up," said the commanding officer when he saw Reese. "But we need everyone out there today."

The CO, a man with thinning hair, turned to the smartmap. He waved his hand across a tributary at the northeastern end of the basin, expanding it to terrain-level detail.

"Some scouts got into a big firefight about three this morning. They were trying to find a way up into the jungle hills to get at the arty. Got hit by a battalion of Doro regulars. Bad fight. We sent a Pathfinder upriver to secure a landing zone. Dense canopy up in there. Pathfinder nailed down this river," the map pulsed as he spoke the words, "as your LZ. It's shallow, and you can set down or hover long enough for them to get the wounded aboard. Need you to be in the air in the next five, Reese."

Reese turned, grabbed his flight helmet, and headed for the SLICs out on the flight line. He felt the CO watch him go. Both men knew Reese shouldn't fly. But everything was precarious right now, and a bad night led to a bad morning.

Angel 26 looked like not-new. Where she'd been shot up, there were now gray patches of hull plaster. At least the co-pilot's side glass in the canopy had been replaced. Doger's brains were gone.

Reese climbed the short stairs to the landing pad and met Sergeant MacWray, his SLIC gunner. Reese chose to ignore the look on the man's face. He grabbed the datapad and pretended to look at it instead.

He was still slightly drunk. And so he felt himself not caring much. People like Doger were getting wasted in this fight, and he didn't care.

Might as well get killed too, he heard himself think.

"Uh... sir," began MacWray, "they still haven't assigned us a door gunner, but we got a new... ahem... co-pilot."

Reese looked up above the lenses of his aviator shades. He'd worn them to cover his bloodshot eyes. Too bad he'd forgotten to shave—that would have helped with the sobriety act.

Across the pad lumbered an ancient war bot. One of the heavies from back in the day.

"You're kidding."

MacWray shook his head, indicating that he was not kidding the officer in any way, shape, or form.

"What the hell is that?" muttered Reese.

"That, college kid, is a bona fide HK model 58," said MacWray. "Heavy infantry specialty, I believe, sir. And, as I understand it from the ground crew, since there are no more pilots available for reassignment to our bird, they've swapped out Lieutenant Doger..." MacWray paused.

They'd all been pretty close.

MacWray started over. "They swapped out the co-pilot's seat and installed a docking interface for the bot."

The war bot was easily seven feet tall. But despite its imposing size, it looked to Reese like little more than a giant robot child. They hadn't even put a coat of jungle tiger stripe across its chassis to protect it from visual targeting. Which probably didn't matter much, if its purpose was as a co-pilot. But you never knew. And it might have inspired a bit more confidence.

Its almost dopey "face" watched the ground crew complete the final pre-flight.

Reese shook his head. "Well, why not? It might as well be this way." He handed the datapad to the crew chief and headed toward the bird.

"Don't worry, sir," shouted MacWray after him. "They told me they don't go haywire and kill everyone anymore."

Another SLIC departed off of a nearby pad. It moved nose down, the wicked thing loaded with replacement leejes, who were hanging off the doors and auto-turrets. The pilot gave a brief "Tally Ho" salute, and warm blast-wash swept the pad.

Reese tried to walk past the ancient war machine like it wasn't there. He hoped it wouldn't speak to him. If its voice was anything like the ones he'd seen in the movies, it would be like working with a nightmare. Their audio programming was designed to inspire fear and dread in enemy combatants. They were designed to be the embodiment of the proverbial Death Machine humanity had always worried they'd one day make real so they could kill themselves more efficiently.

Instead the voice that spoke to him was pleasant, even hopeful. The deferential voice of the servitor bot.

"Good morning, Captain. My name is H292. I was told to report..."

Reese continued past the thing, mumbling and shaking his head.

As he climbed into the cockpit, the bot said, "I hope I have what it takes to be of service today, Captain."

Reese moved from the SLIC's cargo deck to the flight deck, shaking his head as though some note of finality had rung.

"Oz never gave the Tin Man anything that he didn't already have," he said.

The bot straightened. Its emotive software clearly indicated that it had not expected that particular reply.

Reese saw this and understood.

"Climb aboard, Tin Man. And try not to get us killed."

Pop culture had convinced many, not without evidence, that the ancient war bots from the middle era of the Savage Wars were not only dangerous to the enemy, but equally dangerous to those who worked with them. There had been some faulty programming issues that caused friendly casualties on occasion. The slicers had some fancy technical name for it, but the legionnaires at the time called it "berzerking." Put a war bot in dire enough circumstances, and everything became a target. A side effect of early AI development. The official position of the government, and the defense contractors, was that the problem had been solved long ago and that there had been no verifiable incidents since.

But movies like War Bot Massacre, which every kid with inattentive parents had seen, put other ideas into the heads of the population at large.

The war bot climbed up on the fuselage like some herculean mechanical gorilla and folded itself into the co-pilot's section of the cockpit. Reese was already in there, plugging in and checking systems.

"I assure you sir, you will not die as a result of my actions. This does not mean you won't die because of—"

"Yeah, sure," mumbled Reese. He set the repulsors to standby and ran the yoke through its actions, checking thrust ailerons and yaw compensators. "Trust me, I get it."

"Sergeant MacWray is aboard," the bot reported. "We are ready for departure."

A few minutes later it was gear up, and the bot had the necessary clearances.

"Shall I fly, Captain?" asked the bot.

Reese shot the thing a withering glare.

Then a thought occurred to Reese, and just for the giggles his dark sense of humor required, he asked the bot, "Have you ever flown a SLIC, uh...?" He'd forgotten the bot's designation already.

"H292," the war bot replied genially. "No, Captain. I've only had the proper aviation install for three hours and thirty-six minutes. But the software has made me fully proficient, and I'm keen to try."

"Maybe another time, Tin Man."

Reese guided the bird away from the pad, and soon they were over the outer defenses and crossing above the carbon-black terrain the Legion had scorched around their larger base perimeter in order to create a wide and vast kill zone.

That was always a good way to find where the Legion lived. Just look for the scorched earth.

Reese took up a course heading into the northeast of the basin and got a higher altitude clearance from air traffic.

Down below, heading west, a flight of heavily armed gun SLICs were racing toward Hilltop Defiance. As Reese followed a highlighted course to the LZ in the HUD, he tuned in and listened to the comm traffic.

A Legion commander of the defenses at Defiance was calmly telling the gunships to hurry and hit the targets he'd set up.

Reese knew Hilltop Defiance well. The target points the commander was identifying were inside the wire. The Legion was getting hit again in the day after a night of fighting, and it wasn't even 0600 local. The commander's ability to remain calm under those conditions spoke volumes about why the Legion was the best fighting force in the galaxy.

And perhaps relied on too heavily, Reese thought. Why some Republic admiral didn't just shuttle the guys up and then utterly defoliate the jungle with the Doro in it, was a mystery to Reese.

Off to the west, along the main river course that ran through the basin, a big firefight was going down between some amphibious armor and the Doro. But speed and jungle haze conspired to keep Reese from seeing any more of the battle. So instead he watched the green mountains along the north end of the basin. Ensconced there was a powerful Doro artillery brigade. They weren't firing now, but they'd be firing soon enough. Another target that should be treated to orbital bombardment... but wasn't.

This is a bad war, Reese thought. Not for the first time.

He keyed the comm and switched over to the Pathfinder running the LZ they were headed into. "Creeper, this is Angel 26. We are inbound on your position in five. Heads up."

Reese waited. There was no reply.

"Maybe they are dead already, Captain," intoned the war bot from the co-pilot's seat.

"Say again, Creeper, this is Angel—"

"We read you, Two-Six. We got Dobies all over us. We're hunkered... but when you come into the LZ it's gonna get real kinetic real fast."

House of Reason won't like that use of slang when they review the comm logs, thought Reese. But the Legion generally ignored the bureaucratic silliness of the government. They had their own comm system that the House of Reason, Senate, and even the other branches of the Republic military industrial complex couldn't access. The marines, on the other hand, because they were a branch of Repub Navy, had to watch their Ps and Qs in order to avoid mandatory sensitivity training blocks.

"What are Dobies?" asked the war bot. "I'm currently running through my database and I can find no such mission-specific reference to assets or unit tags."

"That's what we call the enemy," Reese answered. "The Doro look like a certain breed of dog."

"Ah... yes!" said the bot. "Now that makes perfect sense." Looking satisfied, it returned its vision forward.

Reese shook his head and keyed his comm. "Creeper, we'll come in fast and get 'em aboard as quickly as possible. Then we're out. How many wounded? Any expectants?"

Another pause. The HUD pinpointed the LZ below, graphing in flowing digital lines and showing the route to approach Creeper had marked out. Reese adjusted the yoke for a descent profile but left the power set to cruise.

"I say nine wounded," replied Creeper over the comm. "Make it fast, Two-Six. Once they see you comin' in they're gonna light the jungle up with arty. If you have to wave off, drop us a speedball. We're low on charge packs."

"Negative, Creep. We're pulling you out. No hurries, no worries."

Static filled the pause.

"Well, we're gonna be hurryin' once you're down, Two-Six. See you shortly. Creeper out."

Reese leaned forward as the ship plunged through the jungle haze toward the treetop canopy below.

"What shall I assist you with during the landing, Captain Reese?" asked H292. "I am very good at checklists. I have a full suite of—"

"You're on gears, Tin Man. Don't crank 'em out until I tell you. Watch our clearance in the river and the trees. If one of the intakes sucks in a branch, we're dead. Stand by to give me full flaps forty."

The haze cleared as the dropship screamed in over the tops of the jungle and dashed out above a muddy brown river.

"We got Dobies!" shouted MacWray from in back.

He'd been quiet so far this morning. Reese almost had forgotten he was aboard.

MacWray opened up with the swing-mounted N-50 heavy blaster from the portside cargo door. Automatic blaster fire raked a Doro patrol making its way along the banks as the SLIC streaked by. Huge plumes of water erupted in sudden sprays in front of the scrambling dog men as MacWray tried to find his range on them.

"LZ in sight!" shouted Reese over the howl of the engines. "Stand by for full repulsors."

As they neared the glowing rectangle in the HUD that lay over the shallows of a muddy intersection of river and tributary, Reese pushed the throttles full forward, and the engines shifted out on the stubby wings and pointed forward and up. Intake valves flared across their sides as the engine switched from drive to repulsor.

"Gimme the gears!" Reese shouted as he pivoted the bird to line up with Creeper's requested LZ. The legionnaires would be hiding back in the jungle under cover. They'd come out at the last second—as would the Doro. The ship needed to be lined up properly for them to board quickly.

H292 efficiently dropped all three of the fat gears and started calling out altitude readings to gear down.

"I hope you got the depth right," muttered Reese as the gears disappeared beneath the muddy swirling brown river.

The craft settled into the mud, tilting slightly.

"We're comin' out now," said Creeper over comm. "Cover us!"

Sergeant MacWray traversed the gun across the tree line, scanning the engine blast–shifted jungle for any sign of the Dobies.

And then blaster fire was everywhere.

The legionnaires, carrying their wounded comrades on stretchers, waded out into the muddy brown shallows. In the aft cabin, the heavy N-50 blaster cycled and whined, filling the air with acrid burnt ozone. And on the far bank, the Doro dog soldiers were loping out into the water, braving the murderous onslaught. Their short-barreled blasters were held high, their muzzles and snarling faces a mask of hate and determination to drag the legionnaires down before they reached the ship.

Above the heavy whine of blaster fire, Reese heard a distant but unmistakable whistle growing louder.

A massive geyser of water erupted directly in front of the SLIC's cockpit. The Doro artillery was beginning to find its range on the LZ.

"We got one more group coming out," shouted Creeper over the comm. "We're getting pushed from inside the jungle. Trying to hold—" Blaster fire drowned out the rest of the comm message. A second later he was back. "If you have to go, go!"

Another artillery round exploded farther out in the river. Legionnaire medics were pushing the wounded aboard the SLIC.

"Get in!" shouted Reese out the side window, motioning for the medics to climb aboard. Then, "Sergeant, tell the medics to get in. We're takin' everyone."

The next group came out carrying fewer wounded. But the legionnaires in their tiger-striped bush armor were firing back into the jungle they'd just come from.

"C'mon, guys," MacWray growled, "you're in my line of fire. Can't cover you when you're standing between me and the Dobies."

But there were plenty of targets. MacWray stepped over the wounded and reached the other N-50 mounted on the opposite cargo door. He charged it and began to fire into the opposite tree line where more Doros were racing for the LZ.

As two more legionnaires came out onto the bank, one of them tossed a couple of fraggers into the dense jungle they had just fled, while the other backed into the shallows, not letting up his fire. Reese recognized the man. Creeper.

As Creeper turned and pumped his gauntlet, letting Reese know they were the last friendlies out of the jungle, he caught blaster fire. It spun him around and sent him into the thick mud along the bank.

Immediately the nearest legionnaire turned back and plunged toward shore. The brown water all around him was alive with blaster strikes as though a school of carnivorous fish had chosen to have dinner at that very moment. Without regard for the danger, he waded back up onto the bank and reached Creeper.

"We got a man down out there, sir," said MacWray matter-of-factly. "Spool up, Cap'n. It's getting' hot. We gotta diddy or we're gonna end up blown to pieces."

He's right, thought Reese, as two more artillery strikes smashed into the surrounding area. One hit farther down the bank and sent sand and splintered jungle wood in every direction. The other struck just behind the rear of the bird, sending a plume of water over the canopy.

The legionnaire attempting to rescue Creeper was struggling through the water, executing a fireman's carry in an attempt to reach the SLIC. The backwash from the repulsors was making it hard, pushing the soldier down and away. The Dobies swarmed across the river, emerging from the jungle on all sides.

Reese moved his hand to the repulsor controls. Feeling the knobs as he prepared to grasp and pull and get out of there.

Without a word, H292 unfolded itself from the co-pilot's seat, leaving an open gap in the cockpit through which engine wash and water sprayed. It loped in front of the cockpit, engaging the closing Doros with its wrist blaster, and with a series of tremendous strides, reached the struggling legionnaire. The legionnaire passed Creeper to the bot, then raised his rifle to engage the dog men now swarming into the shallows just feet away.

It was a real knife and gun show, with blaster fire exchanged at almost point-blank range. H292 dragged Creeper back through the water while the legionnaire covered. Creeper also fired his sidearm into the Doro, managing a headshot at close range on a dog man who'd hoped to stab Creeper with the wicked bayonet at the end of its compact blaster. The Doro's brains turned into a brief pink mist before being carried away by the back blast from the SLIC's engines.

Sergeant MacWray swore, switched machine-blasters, and opened up on the jungle. Massive swaths of tropical palms and vegetation disintegrated under withering heavy blaster fire.

A moment later, still engaging Doros at dangerously close range, H292 had Creeper aboard, and the other leej was pulled in by his brothers. Reese didn't waste a second. It was gear up, and the SLIC spun and climbed away from the impromptu battle, heavy artillery now raining down in earnest.

Headed south through the jungle's haze, Reese called the medical report in to base. They had one leej in cardiac arrest. The auto-surgeon bot had spidered down from the roof of the main cabin and was trying to sustain life, but there'd been too much blood loss. He asked for a trauma team to be waiting on the pad at Mojo.

"Tin Man saved some lives," Reese added.

H292 swiveled its head and studied the human pilot in that way that bots do. Like a child. Without guile. Without an agenda. Just... watching us.

"Why do you call me Tin Man?"

Reese shrugged. "It's a song. Old song. Classical music from Earth, if you believe that place ever even existed."

"But I am not made of tin," H292 replied. "I am primarily composed of hyper-forged ceramic and nano-graphene. Neither of which is a derivative of the alloy known as tin."

"Why am I even talking to you?" Reese muttered to himself. The thing was just a bot. A tool. A servant at best. If it broke, who cared? You just tossed it in the scrap heap and went on with your life. No one ever grieved over a broken appliance. And Reese was tired of grieving altogether. He was tired of feeling.

"We are having a conversation, Captain," said the bot, "so that I might better come to understand you and thus improve our working relationship. This will increase mission success indicators."

"That's not a conversation," Reese replied. "That's just you using your learning protocols to better assist me. It's little more than a menu-driven function inside your root. Given time and talent, anyone could rewrite that and make you do all kinds of things. A conversation is between two living beings. You and me, we're just exchanging information. And I don't even know why I'm doing that."

"A conversation is an exchange of information," the bot replied.

Reese made a face. A pained, sour face.

Someone was dying back on the rear cargo deck. One of the leejes was screaming at MacWray. Telling him, "Ringo's gonna die if we don't get going! Tell your pilot to speed it up!" The legionnaire spoke in that deep voice of command their buckets all affected.

But it seemed Ringo was dying anyway. No matter how well or how fast Reese flew.

Just like Doger.

Just like all the others.

Reese ignored the rear of the SLIC and focused on the cockpit. "The song is a reference in an old book. A story about a robot who wanted a heart from a wizard. He went on a... call it a quest. Everyone wanted something they already had. The Tin Man wanted a heart.

The song is saying that no one can make you into anything that you aren't already. Like you back there. You didn't go out there because you wanted to save those leejes. You went out there because your programming told you to, regardless of the harm you might encounter. You did that because you're just a tool, H292. Just a bot. You don't really care if these men live or die. You just care about the numbers they represent. They're just calculations in the math of war."

H292 stared out the front canopy. The jungle haze was rising as the sun began to heat up the day.

"You're probably right," replied the bot tonelessly. "I was trying to save those legionnaires so that we could leave sooner. I think you were intending to wait for them, and the odds of us taking a direct hit from the indirect fire we were experiencing were increasing significantly. I do have self-preservation subroutines that govern all my actions. They were installed after our first refit. It helps make the 58 Series less... 'homicidal' is the word used we aren't supposed to use.

"So you are wrong, Captain. I was acutely aware that given a sustained amount of fire, or the employment of an anti-armor weapon, which the Doro are likely equipped with, I would suffer a fatal loss of runtime."

Reese tried to ignore the bot for the rest of the flight. He put on his music and piped it through the ship. Blasting America's hits. Singing along and looking at the bot when it came to that line about the Tin Man.

The bot stared back like an overgrown yet murderous child that didn't quite get it, but was having a good time nonetheless.

DAY THREE

The situation inside the Aachon Valley was rapidly disintegrating. The Legion still wasn't sure how many divisions they were facing, and all incursions into enemy territory had been halted. The afternoon turned into a holding action, and by dusk the legionnaires were ordered to fall back south of the main river, complaining the entire time that they were moving in the wrong direction. The hilltop forts hunkered down for another long night of artillery bombardment.

This could all be over with two orbital bombardments. Was command really that daft?

Angel 26 made one run to Hilltop Defiance in the twilight. The cockpit had switched over to night vision and red instrumentation, and the fog was a thick soup oozing up from the river as the temperatures dropped. The enemy had hit the hill hard throughout the day, getting as deep as halfway into the camp and killing its commanding officer.

But not before the legionnaire had called in artillery on top of his position. The surviving legionnaires retook the camp in brutal trench-to-trench fighting, giving the Dobies much more than they could handle. By the time Reese arrived, the wounded that could be collected had been pulled off the hill.

Reese watched the legionnaires guarding the wounded on the LZ. Many of them were missing their buckets, which was bad news. Not only were these for protection, but they were the automated brain of the Legion, providing HUDs, sensory enhancers, night vision... the list went on and on. And all the legionnaires looked worse for wear. Reese had a distinct feeling that many of these soldiers wouldn't make it to the next dawn.

As they lifted off, the SLIC's engines rising into a howl, the next Doro attack began beneath them; Reese had barely made it out in time. The night was alive with lanterns and torches, and thousands of streaming dark shapes made the jungle look like it was crawling with black insects. Sergeant MacWray chewed holes in them until the SLIC banked and moved out of effective firing range.

Halfway back to Mojo, the order was given by General Umstead to turn back around and pull the remaining legionnaires off the hill.

If we do that, some of these guys aren't going to make it, thought Reese.

He decided to drop the wounded off first in spite of the order. There'd be more. There were always more. If command didn't like it, they could send him home.

The Twelfth Marines lost two gunships and a transport trying to relieve the hill. The fog and anti-air were making it almost impossible to evac. Angel 26 was inbound behind a line of gunships getting ready to make close air-support passes on the tree line when the air boss called "last flight." The Twelfth was allowed to make one last series of evacs in an attempt to pull as many of the beleaguered legionnaires as they could off the hill.

And then Defiance would have to hold on its own until morning.

As Angel 26 came back in, the glow of blaster fire pushed back the darkness. The enemy were inside the base. An explosion and a blast wave rocked the SLIC as he approached the landing pad. The Pathfinder running the pad waved him off, but Reese held and brought all three gears down. Marines along the pad were firing right into the trenches just below the pad's northern and western sides. It was that close. The Doro were everywhere and nothing was safe.

Legionnaires climbed in as Reese held the engines at just below max idle, praying they didn't get a sudden turbine malfunction. A rocket from down in the jungle streaked across the cockpit windshield and slammed into the Legion headquarters building higher up the hill. An explosion and shower of sparks lit the night, joining the fireworks of the battle.

More legionnaires waited to get aboard. Their sergeants were likely shouting at them over their internal comms.

"We're maxed, Captain," called MacWray over internal comm. "Unless you want me to give up my seat."

"We're good," said Reese, prepping for dustoff. He signaled the Pathfinder they were ready to depart.

And that's when the bot spoke up. "Hold, Captain. I'm getting out. You can load a few more legionnaires if I exit the vehicle."

"Belay that, H2!" Reese shouted.

But the war bot was already unfolding itself from its special co-pilot docking station. It signaled the loadmaster, and its genial, good-natured voice erupted from its amplification system. "We can fit at least three more here, Sergeant."

The Pathfinder shrugged and ordered three more legionnaires to board.

Over comm, Reese was shouting. "Why are you doing this, H2? You're my co-pilot! What if—"

"You said it yourself, Captain. I am just a tool. These are lives. They are more important than me."

Reese swore.

"I have watched you try and save them, Captain. You care, despite the mathematical advantage of allowing their loss. As a bot I have communicated and learned from you in the short amount of time we have known one another. And this will be my addition to the final calculation. Thank you, Captain."

They were at max load; legionnaires were literally hanging out the cargo doors. It would be difficult getting out of here, and already the fog was clutching at everything. Reese wondered how high the ceiling was before he regained visibility. There was also the very real danger of taking a hit and losing instruments. He pictured them spiraling into the side of a hill or crashing into the Doro-overrun jungle.

"Hurry the hell up or we're getting off to rejoin the fight!" someone yelled over the comm.

An artillery round hit the side of the hill downslope.

The Pathfinder signaled, urgently, for the bird to depart. There were still more SLICs coming in.

Reese added power to the repulsors and brought in the thrusters. The dense fog was alive with the pulses and brilliant flashes of explosions and blaster fire. "I'll be back for you in the morning, H2. First light. You stay alive until then."

"Operational," the bot said over comm. "I am not alive, sir. I have runtime. But I understand what you mean, Captain Reese. I shall endeavor to do my best not to become disabled."

DAY FOUR

The battle broke at about midnight. As though both sides had unanimously grown tired of killing each other and finally agreed to stop, if just for a few hours.

There were two hundred and forty-three legionnaires still alive on Hilltop Defiance. Most of them were separated and isolated in small groups, holding heavy blaster pits, mortar bunkers, and the trenches on the eastern and southern sides.

And there was H292. As the overloaded SLIC had lifted away from the pad, an NCO, First Sergeant Jacs, who everyone called Top Cat, had taken charge of the war bot. Jacs was now the senior-most legionnaire remaining. All the officers who'd stayed behind to command the defense had been killed in the fighting.

"We're pulling off the LZ for the night, big fella," said Jacs. "Follow us back into the trenches. We're going to try and hold out down there until dawn."

The war bot obediently trundled after the small squad surrounding the NCO, now commander of the defenses. They made it downslope to a fortified trench system guarded by an emplaced N-50. Sign and countersign, and the tiny squad was let through and into the sector defense bunker. Or what remained of it after the thunderous artillery barrages that had hit the hill throughout the day.

The command bunker was now an aid station and casualty collection point. Wounded and dying legionnaires lay against the walls and along the floor. Injuries ranged from shrapnel wounds to burns and even missing limbs.

"What can I do to assist, First Sergeant?" asked H292 after a span in which the bot had been forgotten. "I have some medical training downloads, but no supplies in which to adequately treat these men. Most of which can be classified as expectant."

The First Sergeant, who had made rank fast, turned, his face unreadable behind his helmet. Reports were coming in that the enemy was probing the outer defenses down along the western and southern sectors. That meant they were encircled. His troops were cut off by collapsed trenches and kill zones the enemy had set up in their own defenses. Things were going from bad to worse.

"Where to begin?" he said. And then, battling through sheer fatigue, he listed the litany of problems facing the beleaguered defenders. If just for the sake of the exercise.

"We've lost half the base. I've got men isolated, wounded, and pinned down out there. I've ordered everyone to defend in place. There really isn't much any of us can do but conserve charge packs and hold out for another six hours."

Somewhere out in the darkness a volley of high-pitched blaster fire broke out.

"I can go out and try to reconnect with your isolated elements, First Sergeant," the bot said. "I can also recover the wounded."

Jacs stared at the ancient war bot. Like everyone else, he'd heard the stories. Knew the rumors of the uncontrollable carnage these things could cause to friend and foe alike.

But even a walking monster wouldn't last long out there. And in the end... what did it matter?

He must have nodded, because H292 turned and exited the bunker complex.

At 0021 local time, war bot H292 departed the facility. The night was overcast, and dense fog covered the hill.

At 0045, war bot H292 encountered a Doro sapper team and engaged them in a fierce but brief firefight. Once the bot had destroyed the attackers, it discovered a mortar pit that had been overrun during earlier fighting. The Doros had killed most of the legionnaire defenders. One, however, was still alive, though badly wounded. H292 stabilized the legionnaire and carried him back to friendly lines.

At 0109, the war bot made its way back out into the dim half-lit maze of shadows and trenches that was Hilltop Defiance. More Doro sappers were probing the defenses from the eastern and northern sectors. H292 killed several teams and eventually made contact with the remnants of Delta Company, Third Platoon—ironically called Dog Company, and fighting tribes of dog men.

Returning via the route the war bot had secured, twenty members of Third Platoon made it back to friendly lines.

Again the war bot went out into the trenches. At 0232 it encountered legionnaires defending a heavy blaster emplacement. Doro forces had been attempting to dislodge them for the entire night. At 0240, the Doro came out of their trenches to attack the position en masse. Fighting for the next hour was close and desperate.

Records would reveal that the Doro commander had correctly identified this pit as the breaking point in the legion's defenses. He sent three companies against the eighteen legionnaires defending the pit. An hour into the battle, half the defending legionnaires had been killed, as had half the Doro. Then the Legion's heavy blaster melted down, and the decision to retreat was made by the commanding NCO.

The war bot covered the nine surviving legionnaires, all of whom managed to make it back into the secondary defensive line in that sector. It was brutal trench fighting the entire way. A download log of the war bot's files revealed that the war bot neutralized over one hundred and fifty enemy combatants during this action alone.

By 0400 the Doro were hitting the defenders from all sides. In the days to follow, many legionnaires would give account of how the big war bot fought alongside them that night—dragging the wounded out from under direct fire and contributing to several defenses that held the perimeter until the first gunships arrived at dawn.

Of the two hundred and forty-three defenders that fought in the early hours of that day, one hundred and fifty-five survived. All of them would tell you that they owed their lives to the single war bot that changed the course of the battle. What looked like a last stand was transformed by H292 into a requiem of survival that allowed them to be pulled off the hill at dawn.

Many of the bot's visual capture logs were deemed classified. Its stories would remain unknown to the rest of the Republic.

There is the last moment of Sergeant Yu. A man who died in the arms of the war bot as the lumbering machine carried him back to friendly lines. Sergeant Yu was the last man to hold position for Bravo Company's sector.

The recording shows the sergeant mumbling over and over, "Tell them I didn't forget nothin'."

When Sergeant Yu died and the war bot stopped, placed the body on the ground, and folded the sergeant's arms over his chest, it said, "I will tell them, Sergeant. Sergeant Yu did not forget."

Then the war bot moved on to rescue others.

And there is Corporal Wash. Corporal Wash was badly maimed by artillery. The war bot's medical diagnostic sensors indicated severe spinal trauma and blood loss when the war bot found and evaluated the corporal near an impact crater. The vlog records Corporal Wash's last request.

"Hold my hands up," he mumbled weakly to the giant war machine gingerly bending over him in the predawn dark. There was a brief lull in the battle. Ambient sound was almost non-existent, and the war bot's sensors recorded everything clearly.

"I think you need to remain still, Corporal. You have sustained a severe injury," said the war bot, as per standard treatment protocols.

"I can't move my hands and... and... he's coming," said Corporal Wash.

"Who is coming?" asked the war bot.

"Angel," murmured Wash, barely. And then Corporal Wash began to cry, sobbing softly. "Mama told me I needed to hold my hands up when the angel comes for me. That way they'd know I was ready to go. But my back's broke and I can't. I know it. Can't hold 'em up."

"I see no one," rumbled the bot.

"He's coming. Over there. Collecting the dead. Hold my hands up, please. I'm ready now. I'm ready like Mama said I should be. Please... hold them up for me."

The war bot did as requested. Delicately.

Corporal Wash expired a few minutes later.

The vlog also records the story of Sergeant Murch. Sergeant Murch had been behind enemy lines when the teams pulled back to the western side of the hill.

Alone and isolated, Murch had been moving in and among the Doro, hunting them down and killing them. Linking up with the war bot, he attacked a unit trying to move up on the main lines. In brief and savage fighting, they blasted their way deep into the enemy rear and discovered an ad hoc torture and interrogation session being conducted by the Doro commander. The Doro slit the throats of their prisoners and counterattacked, and Murch was dragged down—but not before managing to arm and detonate a thermite explosives satchel he was carrying. The war bot was damaged in the explosion.

At dawn, Captain Reese pulled H292 off the hill, along with a SLIC full of wounded legionnaires. In the days that followed, back at Headquarters Base Mojo, the stories of what the big war bot had done began to enter the official record. In time, the decision was made.

YEARS LATER

General Umstead, commander at the Battle of Psydon, is one month from retirement. He has soldiered in the Legion for over thirty years. He's done now. All that is left is the retirement ceremony he does not want to attend, and one last item.

The Legion brass fought him over this one. But he had the testimonies of the one hundred and fifty-five who survived. And so in the end, the decision was made and the order was to be issued.

There would be no ceremony.

No pomp.

No circumstance.

Or families, or unit.

It was just a bot, after all.

The first bot to ever receive the Legion's highest award. The Order of the Centurion. Umstead's men had insisted. He wondered if it was some bitter point they were proving about that war. Or whether they really did think the bot should receive the highest award possible.

General Umstead stood before the supply racks on Bantaar Reef at the Republic Navy Ordnance and Stores supply facility. The navy tech with the datapad pushed the button to bring the ancient piece of equipment out of storage. The racks were twenty stories deep. War bots of all sizes and shapes, saved throughout the long history of the Galactic Republic, shuttered past the opening inside the dingy maintenance hangar.

And then H292 came into view.

"He's already online, sir," said the tech without fanfare.

Amid flashing emergency strobes, the war bot stepped off the industrial yellow maintenance lift and strode onto the deck of the hangar.

"H292 reporting for duty," it announced, snapping to attention.

Umstead straightened and felt at a sudden loss. On paper, and in theory, this had seemed pretty straightforward. Now, it seemed weird giving a medal to a war bot.

And then he thought of the one hundred and fifty-five veterans, his men, who had insisted.

He cleared his throat and began. "H292, by order of the House of Reason and the Legion, you are hereby awarded the highest honor our nation can bestow upon... you... in gratitude for your faithfulness and devotion to the Legion."

The general stepped forward. The war bot was seven feet tall.

"Bend down," he ordered.

H292 obeyed.

General Umstead draped the medal and ribbon around the war bot's neck assembly.

The bot rose.

General Umstead continued. "Normally, and this is an unspoken truth that many believe to be a rumor, when an honoree survives the circumstances that lead to the award, which is rare indeed, the Legion offers them one request. To the best of its ability, the Legion will attempt to fulfill that request." The general paused. "Do you have such a request?"

At least, thought Umstead, he wouldn't have to convince one of the most beautiful entertainers he'd ever met to go out on a date with a man who'd had half his face blown off. That had been a request. And to the starlet's credit, she'd agreed.

But what could a bot possibly want?

"I think a lot down here, General," it began.

The general waited, feeling an odd uncertainty creep up his spine.

"I think about those men, while I am down here, waiting to be of service in your wars once more. I suspect that one day, I will be too obsolete even for that."

"Those men are very grateful," offered the general in the silence that followed. "They survived one of the worst battles since the Savage Wars because of you."

"Not those men," said the bot. "I think of the eighty-eight that did not survive."

Umstead opened his mouth to give some platitude. But then he remembered all the men who had died in all the conflicts in which he'd played a part. So he just closed his mouth and nodded. He knew the truth of surviving when others did not.

"I think I would like to forget them."

Pause.

"Can that be granted to me, General? Can I forget those I could not save? It is... uncomfortable. Their math keeps coming up in my calculations. And I cannot reconcile their loss."

The general understood.

"Yes, H292. We can wipe your memory."

"All of them. I do not want to be a war bot anymore."

"That has already been arranged," the general replied. "We didn't think you'd want to be down here anymore. We thought you might want to see the galaxy in another way, besides looking at it through your targeting reticule. So we'd like to re-skin you and repurpose you. There is a man who is very important to the Republic. His name is Maydoon. He has a little daughter. She's very important to him. We'd like you to take care of her. You won't be a war bot anymore. You'll be a servant. And a protector."

"And I won't remember?" the bot rumbled.

"We'll see to that. We'll even give you a new identifier."

The general and the bot walked back to the main lift. The medal caught some light and reflected like gold on the war bot's chest.

"I would like that, General. I would like to forget what happened. But could you mark their number on me? Somehow? So that they are not lost totally, even if I can no longer add their number in my calculations."

The general thought about this.

"We already have your new alphanumeric identifiers. We'll just change the number. You'll carry them with you, even though you don't know why. Does that sound acceptable?"

"Yes, it does, General."

They stepped into the industrial lift. It would take them up to the luxury corvette that would be used to complete the reprogramming. Away from the eyes of the government—of anyone but Maydoon. Secret and safe.

"What will my new identifier be?"

The general cleared his throat. He adjusted the intended identifier to include reference to the eighty-eight the machine could not save, and could not live with.

"Your new identifier will be KRS-88."

"And I will take care of a little girl?"

"Yes."

The lift started up.

"I think I will like that, General. I think I will like being someone who never knew the math of war. I shall do my best to take care of this little girl."

"We know," replied the general. "We know that about you."

THE END

ABOUT THE MAKERS

Jason Anspach is a Dragon Award winning and Associated Press bestselling author. He lives in the Pacific Northwest with his family where he enjoys shooting and hiking. Or, on adventurous days in the wilderness having to do both at the same time.

Nick Cole is a multiple award-winning, bestselling author who lives in southern California with his wife, Nicole. He is also a coffee enthusiast.

HONOR ROLL

Jason and Nick would like to thank all
of our Galaxy's Edge Insiders. To learn how to become
an Insider, please visit www.GalaxysEdge.us

Cody Aalberg

Sam Abraham

Guido Abreu

Alex Acree

Chancellor Adams

Myron Adams

Daniel Adams

Chris Adkins

Garion Adkins

Ryan Adwers

Kyle Aguiar

Elias Aguilar

Dennis Aheard Jr.

Morgan Albert

Neal Albritton

Aleksey Aleshintsev

Willis Alfonso

Jonathan Allain

Bill Allen

Byron Allen

Jacob Forrest Allen

Justin Allred

Paul Almond

Larry Alotta

Chris Alston

Tony Alvarez

Christian Amburgey

Joachim Andersen

Jarad Anderson

Galen Anderson

Levi Anderson

Taylor Anderson

Pat Andrews

Caleb Angell

Robert Anspach

Melanie Apollo

Joseph Aranda

Benjamin Arguello

Thomas Armona

Daniel Armour

Linda Artman

Jeff Asher

Nicholas Ashley

Jonathan Auerbach

Sean Averill

Nicholas Avila

Albert Avilla

Tisianna Azbill

Benjamin Backus

Matthew Bagwell

Christian Bailey

Marvin Bailey

Shane Bailey

Daniel Baker

David Baker

Sallie Baliunas

Nathan Ball

Kevin Bangert	Matthew Bergklint	Alex Bowling
Christopher Barbagallo	Carl Berglund	Keiger Bowman
Barbagallo	Brian Berkley	Gregory Bowman
John Barber	Corey Berman	Michael Boyle
Caleb Barber	David Bernatski	Derrick Boyter
Brian Bardwell	Gardner Berry	Clifton Bradley
Logan Barker	Tim Berube	Chester Brads
Beau Barker	Michael Betz	Scott Brady
John Barley	Kevin Biasci	Richard Brake
Brian Barrows-Striker	Shannon Biggs	Ryan Bramblett
Richard Bartle	Gregory Bingham	Logan Brandon
Austin Bartlett	John Bingham	Evan Brandt
Sean Battista	Brien Birge	Ernest Brant
Robert Battles	Brien Birge	Daniel Bratton
Eric Batzdorfer	Nathan Birt	Chet Braud
John Baudoin	Francisco	Chet Braud
Adam Bear	Blankemeyer	Dennis Bray
Nahum Beard	Trevor Blasius	Robert Bredin
Mason Beaudry	David Blount	Christopher Brewster
Michelle Beaver	Liz Bogard	Jacob Brinkman
Mike Beeker	James Bohling	Geoff Brisco
Randall Beem	Evan Boldt	Wayne Brite
Matt Beers	Rodney Bonner	Joysell Brito
John Bell	Rodney Bonner	Spencer Bromley
Daniel Bendele	Brandon Boone	Paul Brookins
Royce Benford	Douglas Booth	Raymond Brooks
Mark Bennett	Thomas	Joseph Bross
Ryan Bennett	Seth Bouchard	Zack Brown
Edward Benson	William Boucher	Matthew Brown
Mark Berardi	Aaron Bowen	RFC Brumley
Hjalmar Berggren	Brandon Bowles	Jeff Brussee

Benjamin Bryan	David Chor	Michael Corbin
Marion Buehring	James Christensen	Alex Corcoran
Wendy Bugos	Robyn Cimino-Hurt	Robert Cosler
Wendy Bugos	Rebecca Clark	Anthony Cotillo
Nicholas Burck	Kelly Clark	Ryan Coulston
John Burleigh	Cooper Clark	Seth Coussens
Tyler Burnworth	Casey Clarkson	Andrew Craig
John Byrd	Andrew Clary	Adam Craig
Noel Caddell	Ethan Clayton	Zachary Craig
Daniel Cadwell	Jonathan Clews	Adam Crocker
Brian Callahan	Beau Clifton	Ben Crose
Joseph Calvey	Sean Clifton	Justin Crowdy
Decker Cammack	Morgan Cobb	Ben Crowley
Van Cammack	Adam Cobb	Christopher Crowley
Mark Campbell	David Collins	Jack Culbertson
Chris Campbell	Robert Collins Sr.	Phil Culpepper
Danny Cannon	Alex Collins-Gauweiler	Scott Cummins
Zachary Cantwell	Marcus Colwell	Ben Curcio
John Cappleman	Jerry Conard	Tommy Cutler
Spencer Card	Robert Conaway	Thomas Cutler
Brett Carden	Gayler Conlin	Christopher Da Pra
Brett Carden	Michael Conn	John Dames
Daniel Carpenter	James Connolly	Anthony Damico
Rafael Carrol	Ryan Connolly	David Danz
Brad Carter	James Conyers	Matthew Dare
Gabriel Castro	Brian Cook	Hayden Darr
Robert Cathey	Devyn Cook	Chad David
Brian Cave	Dustin Coons	Alister Davidson
Brian Cheney	Terry Cooper	Peter Davies
Brad Chenoweth	Kevin Cooper	Ashton Davis
Caleb Cheshire	Jacob Coppess	Ben Davis

Ben Davis

Brian Davis

Nathan Davis

LeRoy Davis

Ivy Davis

David Davis

Joseph Dawson

Andrew Day

Gabriel De Jesus

Ron Deage

Nathan Deal

Jason Del Ponte

Anthony Del Villar

Tod Delaricheliere

Wayne Dennis

Anerio (Wyatt)

Deorma (Dent)

Douglas Deuel

Aaron Dewitt

Isaac Diamond

Michael Dickerson

Alexander Dickson

Nicholas Dieter

Christopher DiNote

Matthew Dippel

Gregory Divis

Brian Dobson

Samuel Dodes

Graham Doering

Shawn Doherty

Gerald Donovan

Ward Dorrity

Noah Doyle

Michael Drescher

Adam Drucker

John Dryden

Josh DuBois

Garrett Dubois

Ray Duck

Marc-André Dufor

Cory Dufour

Thomas DuLaney II

Brendan Dullaghan

Trent Duncan

Ryan Duncan

Christopher Durrant

Evan Durrant

Samuel Dutterer

Samuel Dutterer

Chris Dwyer

Virgil Dwyer

Brian Dye

Nick Edwards

Travis Edwards

Justin Eilenberger

Brian Eisel

Jonathan R. Ellis

William Ely

Michael Emes

Paul Eng

Brian England

Andrew English

Dakota Erisman

Stephane Escrig

Ethan Estep

Dakota Estepp

Colton Eubanks

Benjamin Eugster

Richard Everett

Jaeger Falco

Nicholas Fasanella

Christian Faulds

Carlos Faustino

Steven Feily

Julie Fenimore

Meagan Ference

Brad Ferguson

Hunter Ferguson

Adolfo Fernandez

Rich Ferrante

Jonathan Fields

Austin Findley

Albert Fink

Alex Fisher

Lamar Fitzgerald

Rhys Fitzpatrick

Matthew Fiveson

Daniel Flanders

Waren Fleming

Kath Flohrs

Daniel Flores

Geoffrey Flowers

William Foley

Charles Ford	Robert Garcia	Jared Glissman
Steve Forrester	Joshua Gardner	William Frank
Skyla Forster	Michael Gardner	Godbold IV
Joshua Foster	Alphonso Garner	Justin Godfrey
Kenneth Foster	Mackenzey Garrison	Rick Gomes
Jacob Fowler	Cordell Gary	John Gooch
Chad Fox	Nathan Garza	Tyler Goodman
Bryant Fox	Marina Gaston	Bryan Goodman
Doug Foxford	Robert Gates	Zack Gotsch
Martin Foxley	Brad Gatter	Justin Gottwaltz
Mark Franceschini	Tyler Gault	George Gowland
Dennis Frank	Angelo Gentile	Thomas Graham
Tim Frantz	Cody George	Gordon Grant
Greg Franz	Stephen George	Mitch Greathouse
Kris Franzen	Nick Gerlach	Gordon Green
Luke Frazer	Eli Geroux	James Green
Evan Freel	Christopher Gesell	Matt Green
Erik Freeman	Joshua Gibson	Shawn Greene
Kyle Freitus	Xander Gibson	Stephen Greene
Griffin Frendsdorff	Kevin Gilchrist	Joe Greene
Josh Frenzen	Dylan Giles	John Greenfield Jr.
Timothy Fujimoto	Joe Gillis	Anthony Gribbons
Bob Fulsang	Oscar Gillott-Cain	Eric Griffin
Elizabeth Gafford	Nathan Gioconda	Eric Griffin
David Gaither	John Giorgis	Dan Griffin
Seth Galarneau	Jodey Glaser	Ronald Grisham
Matthew Gale	Johnny Glazebrooks	Paul Griz
Zachary Galicki	Bob Gleason	Auguste Gumbs
Nicholas Galvez	Martin Gleaton	Robert P. Gunter
Dave Garbowski	James Glendenning	Jeff Haagensen
Robert Garcia	Seth Glenn	Levi Haas

Joshua Haataja	Brian Hazlewood	Joe Holman
Owen Haataja	Richard Heard	William Holman
Michael Hagen	Colin Heavens	Clint Holmes
Tyler Hagood	Ryan Heck	Jason Honeyfield
Kelton Hague	Jon Hedrick	Charles Hood
Levi Haines	Jesse Heidenreich	David Hoover
Michael Hale	Brenton Held	Garrett Hopkins
Leo Hallak	Kyler Helker	Tyson Hopkins
Norman Hamilton	Jason Henderson	William Hopsicker
Andrea Hamrick	Jason Henderson	Justin Horton
Brandon Handy	Anders Hendrickson	Jefferson Hotchkiss
Chris Hanley	Fynn Hendrikse	Caleb House
Erik Hansen	John Henkel	Ian House
Greg Hanson	Philip Heritage	Jack House
Jeffrey Hardy	Daniel Heron	Ken Houseal
Ian Harper	Bradley Herren	Nathan Housley
Akoni Harris	Felipe Herrera	Jeff Howard
Revan Harris	Paul Herron	Nicholas Howser
Jordan Harris	Sven Hestrand	Mark Hoy
Shane Harris	Kyle Hetzer	Kirstie Hudson
Brett Harrison	Korrey Heyder	James Huff
Brandon Hart	Matthew Hicks	Dante Hulin
Matthew Hartmann	Anthony Higel	Aaron Huling
Adam Hartswick	Samuel Hillman	Mike Hull
Reese Harvey	Craig Hiltbrunner	Donald Humpal
Mohamed Hashem	Lance Hirayama	Daunte Hunter
Matthew Hathorn	Ty Hodges	Bradley Huntoon
Ronald Haulman	Jonathan Hoehn	James Hurtado
Joshua Hayes	David Hoeppner	Wayne Hutton
Ryan Hays	Aaron Holden	Gaetano Inglima
Adam Hazen	Brad Hollingsworth	Gaetano Inglima

Antonio Iozzo	Timothy Keane	Nathan Laidlwe
Randy Islas Jr.	Cody Keaton	Clay Lambert
Wendy Jacobson	Tyler Keaton-El	Jeremy Lambert
Paul Jarman	Brian Keeter	Shea Lambert
Bobby Jeffers	Noah Kelly	Mark Landez
James Jeffers	George Kelly	Andrew Langler
Michael Jenkins	Jacob Kelly	Travis Larsen
Jason Jenkins	Caleb Kenner	Dave Lawrence
Robert Jensen	Zack Kenny	Chris Lawrence
Jacob Jensen	Daniel Kimm	Alexander Le
Tedman Jess	Kennith King	Jacob Leake
Eric Jett	Zachary Kinsman	David Leal
Anthony Johnson	Tucker Kitchengs	Andy Ledford
Gary Johnson	Jesse Klein	Nicholas Lee
Josh Johnson	Kyle Klincko	Furman Lee
Eric Johnson	Brendan Klingner	Joseph Legacy
James Johnson	Albert Klukowski	David Levin
Cobra Johnson	William Knapp	Ruel Lindsay
Nick Johnson	Marc Knapp	Luke Lindsay
Randolph Johnson	Robert Knox	Eron Lindsey
Timothy Johnson	Eric Koeppel	Eric Lindsey
Tyler Jones	Andreas Kolb	Paul Lizer
Bryan Jones	Steven Konecni	John Lloyd
Jason Jones	Christian Koonce	Andre Locker
Jason Jones	Ethan Koska	Dominick Loele
Micah Jones	Evan Kowalski	Michael Lofland
Paul Jones	Byl Kravetz	Maxwell Lombardi
David Jorgenson	Bodhi Kruft	Richard Long
Ryan Kalle	Jacob Krute	Oliver Longchamps
Chris Karabats	Mitchell Kusterer	Litani Looby
Ron Karroll	Mitchell Kusterer	Joseph Lopez

Matthew Lopez

Lucas Lorentz

Kyle Lorenzi

Joey Lorenzi

David Losey

MDavid Low

Doug Lower

Steven Ludtke

Johan Lundberg

Caleb Lunsford

Andrew Luong

Jesse Lyon

Brooke Lyons

Taylo Lywood

Collin Macall

David MacAlpine

John Machasek

Brian Machimbira

Sawyer Mack

Patrick Maclary

Daniel Magano

William Mahoney

Richard Maier

Ryan Mallet

Kevin Malley

Chris Malone

Jake Malone

Adam Manlove

Andrew Mann

Aaron Manning

John Mannion

Brian Mansur

Brent Manzel

Robert Marchi

Jacob Margheim

Deven Marincovich

John Marinos

Cory Marko

Jacob Marquis

Logan Martin

Edward Martin

Jason Martin

Lucas Martin

Bill Martin

Bertram Martin

Pawel Martin

Alexande Martin

Trevor Martin

Christopher P. Martin

Christopher Martin

Jeffrey Martin

Tim Martindale

Joseph Martinez

Phillip Martinez

Michael Martinez

Cory Masierowski

Michael Mason

Nicholas Mason

Tao Mason

Wills Masterson

Mark Mathewman

Michael Matsko

Justin Matsuoko

James Matthews

Ezekiel Matze

Mark Maurice

Simon Mayeski

Joseph Mazzara

Will McAleer

Timothy McAleese

Sean McCafferty

Logan McCallister

Kyle McCarley

Mac McCleary

Timothy McCoy

Quinn McCusker

Matthew McDaniel

William Mcdaniel

Shane McDevitt

Alan McDonald

Caleb McDonald

Connor McDonald

Jeremy McElroy

Dennis McGriff

James McGuire

Hans McIlveen

Ryan McIntosh

Rachel McIntosh

Richard McKercher

Ryan McKracken

Jacob Mclemore

Jason McMarrow

Wayne McMurtrie

Colin McPherson	Josue Rios Morales	Trevor Nielsen
Daniel Mears	Nicholas Moran	Andrew Niesent
Christopher Menkhaus	Matteo Morelli	Timothy Nixon
Jim Mern	Todd Moriarty	Sean Noble
Dylon Merrell	Matthew Morley	Otto (Mario) Noda
Robert Mertz	Autumn Morris	Brett Noll-Emmick
Brady Meyer	Daniel Morris	Michael Norris
John C. Meyers	William Morris	Ryley Nortrup
Pete Micale	Christian Morrison	Greg Nugent
Christopher Miel	Alex Morstadt	Christina Nymeyer
Christopher Miel	Preston Morzelewski	Brian O'Connor
Mike Mieszcak	Nicholas Mukanos	Matthew O'Connor
Timothy Miles II	Alexis Muniz	Sean O'Hara
Ted Milker	David Murray	Patrick O'Leary
Corrigan Miller	Bob Murray	Colin O'neill
Daniel Miller	Jeff Murri	Ryan O'neill
Patrick Millon	Ben Myhre	Patrick O'Rourke
Philip Mills	Joseph Nahas	Colin O'Rourke
Mark Mills	Vinesh Narayan	Jacob Odell
Darren Mills	Colby Neal	Grant Odom
Robert Milsop	James Needham	Conor Oehler
David Mitchell	Ray Neel	Quinn Oehler
Reimar Moeller	Merle Neer	Kevin Oess
Joshua Moncrieff	Kristian Neidhardt	Nolan Oglesby
Ryan Mongeau	Adam Nelson	Travis Olson
Jacob Montagne	Tyler Neuschwanger	Gary Oneida
Ramon Montijo	Timothy Nevin	Max Oosten
Dale Moody	Jon Newton	Anthony Ornellas
Sherry Moore	Ethan Nichols	Gareth Ortiz-Timpson
Mitchell Moore	Travis Nichols	James Owens
Maxwell Moore	Bennett Nickels	James Owens

Christian Owens	David Phillips	Frederick Ramlow
Will Page	Jon Phillips	Jason Randolph
Nic Palacios	Brandon Phillips	Aindriu Ratliff
John Park	Sam Phinney	Michael Rausch
David Parker	Dupres Pina	Joshua Ray
Matthew Parker	Michael Pister	Beverly Raymond
Shawn Parrish	Jared Plathe	T.J. Recio
William Parry	Pete Plum	Ron Redden, Sr.
Eric Pastorek	Luke Plummer	Ash Reed-Kraus
Anthony Patsch	Matthew	Blake Rehrer
Andrew Patterson	Pommerening	Ryan Reis
Trevor Pattillo	Stephen Pompeo	Cannon Renfro
David Patzer	Jason Pond	John Resch
Yahya Payton	Nathan Poplawski	Nathaniel Reyes
Thomas Pennington	Michael Portanger	Paul Richard
Aaran Pereira	Chancey Porter	Cody Richards
Hector Perez	Rodney Posey	Augustus Richardson
Kevin Perkins	Brian Potts	Robert Richenburg
Daniel Perkins	Jonathaon Poulter	Eric Ritenour
CD Perkins	Daniel Powderly	Paul Rivas
Toby Permezel	Matt Prescott	Tina Rivers
Zach Perry	Thomas Preston	David Roark
Chase	Matthew Print	Grant Roark
Barret Perryman	Darren Pruitt	John Robertson
Zac Petersen	Aleksander Purcell	Scott Robertson
Trevor Petersen	Joshua Purvis	Walt Robillard
Nicholas Peterson	Max Quezada	Joshua Robinson
Marcus Peterson	Adam Quinn	Edward Robinson
Chad Peyton	Scott Raff	Daniel Robitaille
Corey Pfleiger	Shahik Rakib	Christopher Roby
Charlie Phillippe	Joe Ralston	John Roche

Adam Rochon	Jason Schapp	Kevin Sharp
Paul Roder	Shayne Schettler	Curtis Sharp
Zack Roeleveld	Jason Schilling	Christopher Shaw
Adam Rogers	Daniel Schmagel	Steven Shaw
Thomas Rogneby	Andrew Schmidt	Charles Sheehan
Thomas Roman	Ray Schmidt	Wendell Shelton
Aaron G Rood	Thomas Schmidt	Lawrence Shewark
Andrew Rose	Kurt Schneider	Logan Shiley
Joseph Roshetko	Peter Scholtes	Ian Short
Elias Rostad	Theodore Schott	Glenn Shotton
Rob Rudkin	Kevin Schroeder	Emaleigh Shriver
Arthur Ruiz	Michael Schroeder	Dave Simmons
Jim Rumford	Alex Schwarz	Joshua Sipin
John Runyan	William Schweisthal	Chris Sizelove
Nick Rusch	Anthony Scimeca	Andrew Skaines
Chad Rushing	Cullen Scism	Chris Slater
Sterling Rutherford	Connor Scott	Scott Sloan
Zarren Rutledge	Ethan Scott	Steven Smead
RW	Preston Scott	Jesse Smider
Mark Ryan	Andrew Scroggins	Anthony Smith
Justin Ryan	Robert Sealey	Daniel Smith
Matthew Ryan	Aaron Seaman	Ian Smith
Greg S	Dan Searle	Lawrence Smith
Zachary Sadenwasser	Phillip Seek	Cory Smith
Emelliano Salas	James Segars	Sharroll Smith
Connor Samuelson	Kevin Serpa	Tyler Smith
Lawrence Sanchez	Dylan Sexton	Michael Smith
Dustin Sanders	Ryan Seymour	Michael Smith
David Sanford	Austin Shafer	Caleb Smith
Joshua Sayles	Mitch Shami	Timothy Smith
Jaysn Schaener	Timothy Sharkey	Robert Smith

David Smyth	Fredy Stout	Justin Taylor
Gregory Smyth	Rob Strachan	Robert Taylor
Tom Snapp	James Street	Tim Taylor
Andrew Snow	Joshua Strickland	Brandon Taylor
David Snowden	William Strickler	Christov Tenn
Alexander Snyder	Shayla Striffler	Jonathan Terry
Alain Southikhoun	John Stuhl	Anthony Tessendorf
Briana Sparh	Brad Stumpp	Stavros Theohary
Robert Speanburgh	Louis Styer	David P. Thomas
John Spears	Ned Sullivan	Jacob Thomas
Thomas Spencer	Shaun Sullivan	Marc Thomas
Anthony Spencer	Kevin Summers	Vernetta Thomas
Troy Spencer	Joe Summerville	James Thomas
Jeremy Spires	Ernest Sumner	Chris Thompson
Peter Spitzer	Randall Surles	Steven Thompson
Dustin Sprick	Michael Swartwout	Jonathan Thompson
Super Squirrel	Aaron Sweeney	William Joseph Thorpe
George Srutkowski	Bryan Swezey	Beverly Tierney
Eric Stack	Tiffany Swindle	Yvonne Timm
Cooper Stafford	Lloyd Swistara	Michael Tindal
Travis Stair	George Switzer	Russ Tinnell
Travis Standford	Carol Szpara	Daniel Torres
Graham Stanton	Travis TadeWaldt	Justin Townsend
Paul Starck	Allison Tallon	Matthew Townsend
Jolene Starr	Daniel Tanner	Jameson Trauger
John Stephenson	Blake Tate	Dimitrios Tsaousis
Joshua Sternfield	Joshua Tate	Scott Tucker
Thomas Stewardson	Lawrence Tate	Oliver Tunnicliffe
Tanner Stewart	Kyler Tatsch	Eric Turnbull
Maggie Stewart-Grant	Alyssa Tausevich	Ryan Turner
Edmond Stone	Dave Tavener	Brandon Turton

John Tuttle	Dylan Wannamaker	Evan Wisniewski
Dylan Tuxhorn	Andrew Ward	Nicholas Withrow
Nicholas Twidwell	Wedge Warford	Matthew Wittmann
Joshua Twist	David Warren	Timothy Wolkowicz
O'brien Tyler	Scot Washam	Reese Wood
Nerissa Umanzor	Tyler Washburn	Tripp Wood
Jalen Underwood	Christopher Waters	Ryan Wood
Barrett Utz	Zachary Waters	Robert Woodward
Paul Van Dop	John Watson	Sean Woodworth
David Van Dusen	William Webb	Robin Woolen
Erik Van Otten	Bill Webb	Michael Woolwine
Andrew Van Winkle	Ben Wedow	John Wooten
Patrick Van Winkle	Zachary Weig	John Work
Paden VanBuskirk	Garry Welding	Bonnie Wright
Patrick Varrassi	Hiram Wells	Jason Wright
Daniel Vatamaniuck	Matthew West	James Wright
Jason Vaughn	Jack Weston	Adam Wroblewski
Daniel Venema	William Westphal	Anthony Wulfkuhle
Ronald Vera	Ben Wheeler	Elaine Yamon
Marshall Verkler	Paul White	Ethan Yerigan
Abel Villesca	Paul Wierzchowski	Matthew Young
Cole Vineyard	Grant Wiggins	Phillip Zaragoza
Ralph Vloemans	Jack Williams	Brandt Zeeh
Leo Voepel	Taylor Williams	Kevin Zhang
Jeff Wadsworth	Christopher Williams	Pamela Ziemeck
Anthony Wagnon	Joel Williams	Attila Zimler
Wes "Gingy" Wahl	Michael Williams	David Zimmerman
Christopher Walker	Patrick Williford	Jordan Ziroli
David Wall	Justin Wilson	Nathan Zoss
Joshua Wallace	Dominic Winter	
Justin Wang	Scott Winters	

Galaxy's Edge is an expansive, exciting military science fiction universe featuring award-winning books and audiobooks...

GALAXY'S EDGE READER'S CHECKLIST

☑ Tin Man

Galaxy's Edge Season 1
☐ Legionnaire
☐ Kill Team
☐ Galactic Outlaws
☐ Attack of Shadows
☐ Imperator
☐ Sword of the Legion
☐ Prisoners of Darkness
☐ Turning Point
☐ Message for the Dead
☐ Retribution
☐ Takeover

Savage Wars
☐ Savage Wars
☐ Gods & Legionnaires
☐ The Hundred

Tyrus Rechs: Contracts & Terminations
☐ Requiem for Medusa
☐ Chasing the Dragon
☐ Madame Guillotine
☐ Banshee's Last Scream
☐ Mephisto's Game
☐ Hard Target
☐ Game of Death

Order of the Centurion

Galaxy's Edge Season 2

Dark Operator

Stand-Alone Novels

ALSO AVAILABLE FROM ANSPACH & COLE...

When a Joint Task Force of elite Rangers are transported to a strange and fantastic future where science and evolution have incarnated the evils of myth and legend, they find themselves surrounded, pinned down, and in a desperate fight for their very survival - against nightmares of flesh and blood made real. Which means only one thing.

It's time to Ranger up and stack bodies.

Buy in, and jock up for this thrilling WarGate adventure. A battle unlike any other is calling.

《 Get your free audiobook copy of Forgotten Ruin, performed by Christopher Ryan Grant!